SO-AVT-458

KAY THOMPSON'S ELOISE

Eloise's New Bonnet

STORY BY Lisa McClatchy

ILLUSTRATED BY Tammie Lyon

Ready-to-Read

Simon Spotlight
New York   London   Toronto   Sydney   New Delhi

SIMON SPOTLIGHT

An imprint of Simon & Schuster Children's Publishing Division

1230 Avenue of the Americas, New York, NY 10020

First Simon Spotlight hardcover edition December 2016

First Aladdin Paperbacks edition January 2007

For information about special discounts for bulk purchases, please contact Simon & Schuster
Special Sales at 1-866-506-1949 or business@simonandschuster.com.

The text of this book was set in Century Old Style.

Manufactured in the United States of America 1116 LAK

2 4 6 8 10 9 7 5 3 1

The Library of Congress has cataloged a previous edition as follows:

Library of Congress Cataloging-in-Publication Data

McClatchy, Lisa.

Eloise's new bonnet / story by Lisa McClatchy ; illustrated by Tammie Lyon.—1st Aladdin
Paperbacks ed.

p. cm.—(Kay Thompson's Eloise) (Ready-to-read)

"Artwork in the style of Hilary Knight"—T.p. verso.

Summary: Eloise tries on various hats until Nanny gives her the perfect one.

[1. Hats—Fiction. 2. Plaza Hotel (New York, N.Y.)—Fiction. 3. Hotels, motels, etc.—Fiction.
4. New York (N.Y.)—Fiction.] I. Lyon, Tammie, ill. II. Thompson, Kay, 1911– III. Title. IV.
Series. V. Series: Ready-to-read.

PZ7.M47841375Elo 2007

[E]—dc22

2006012228

ISBN 978-1-4814-7677-5 (hc)

ISBN 978-0-689-87452-9 (pbk)

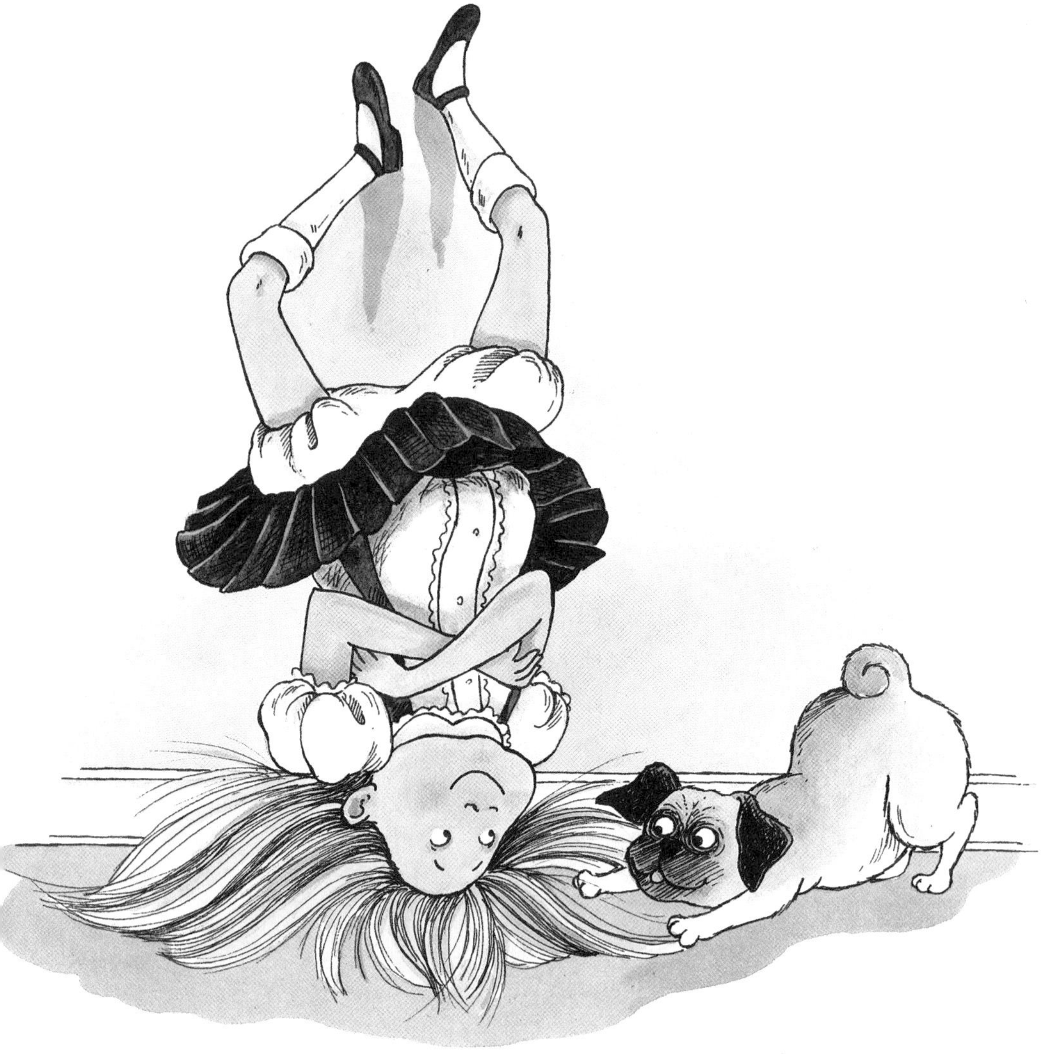

I am Eloise.
I am six.
I live in The Plaza hotel
on the tippy-top floor.

I have a dog.
His name is Weenie.

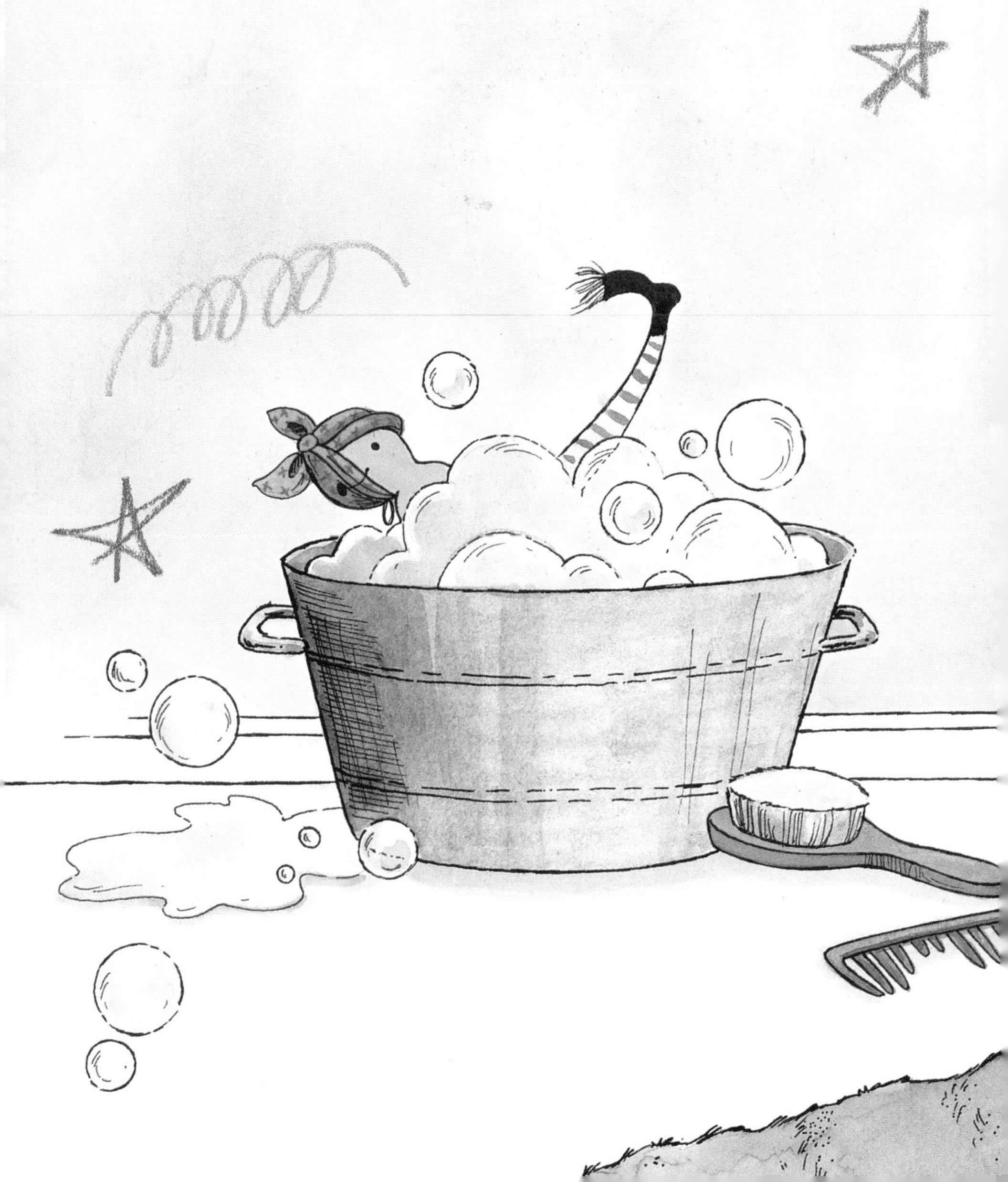

Here is what I like to do:
put sunglasses on Weenie.

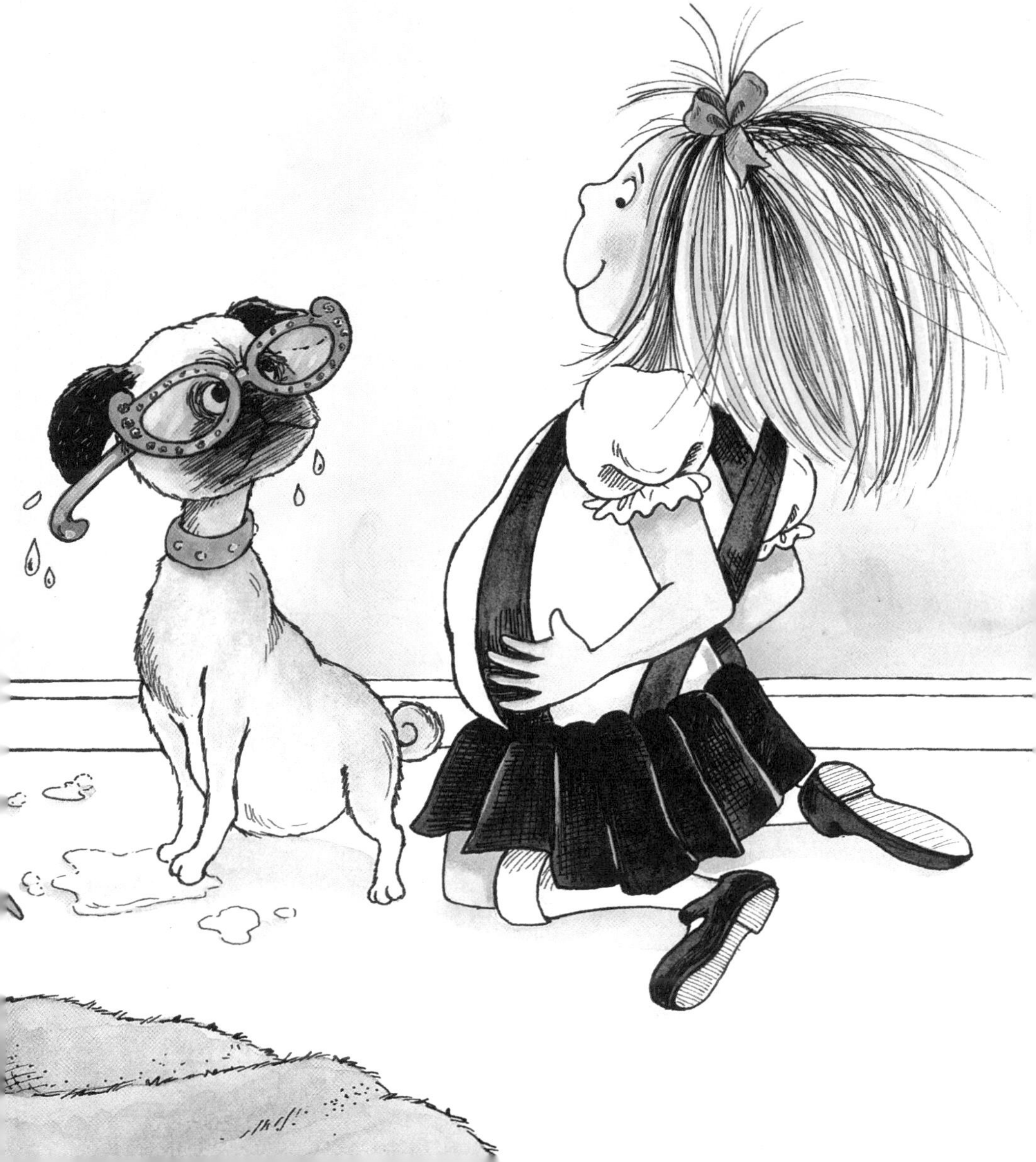

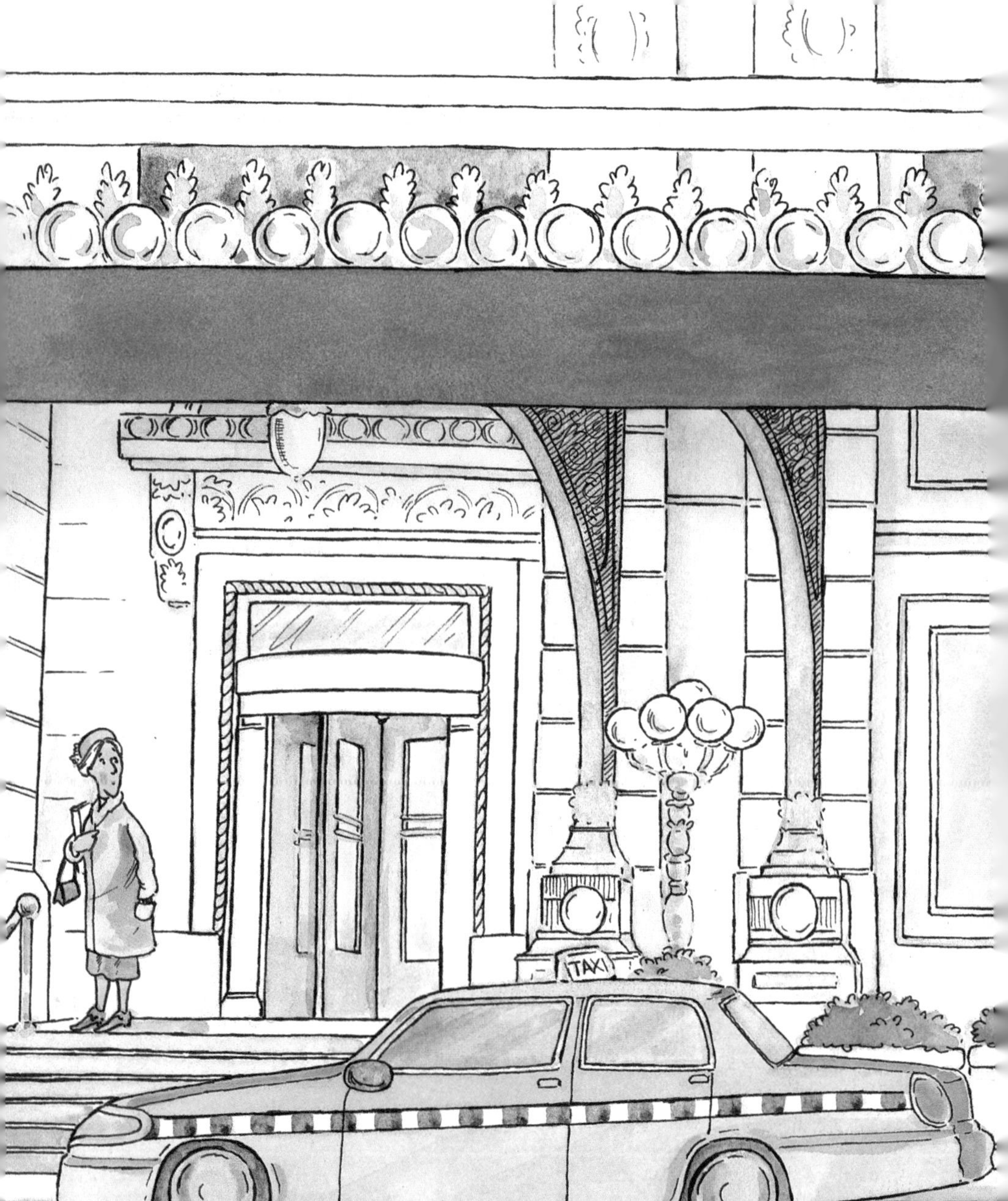
TAXI

Today the sun is shining.
Spring has sprung.
I put my sunglasses on too.

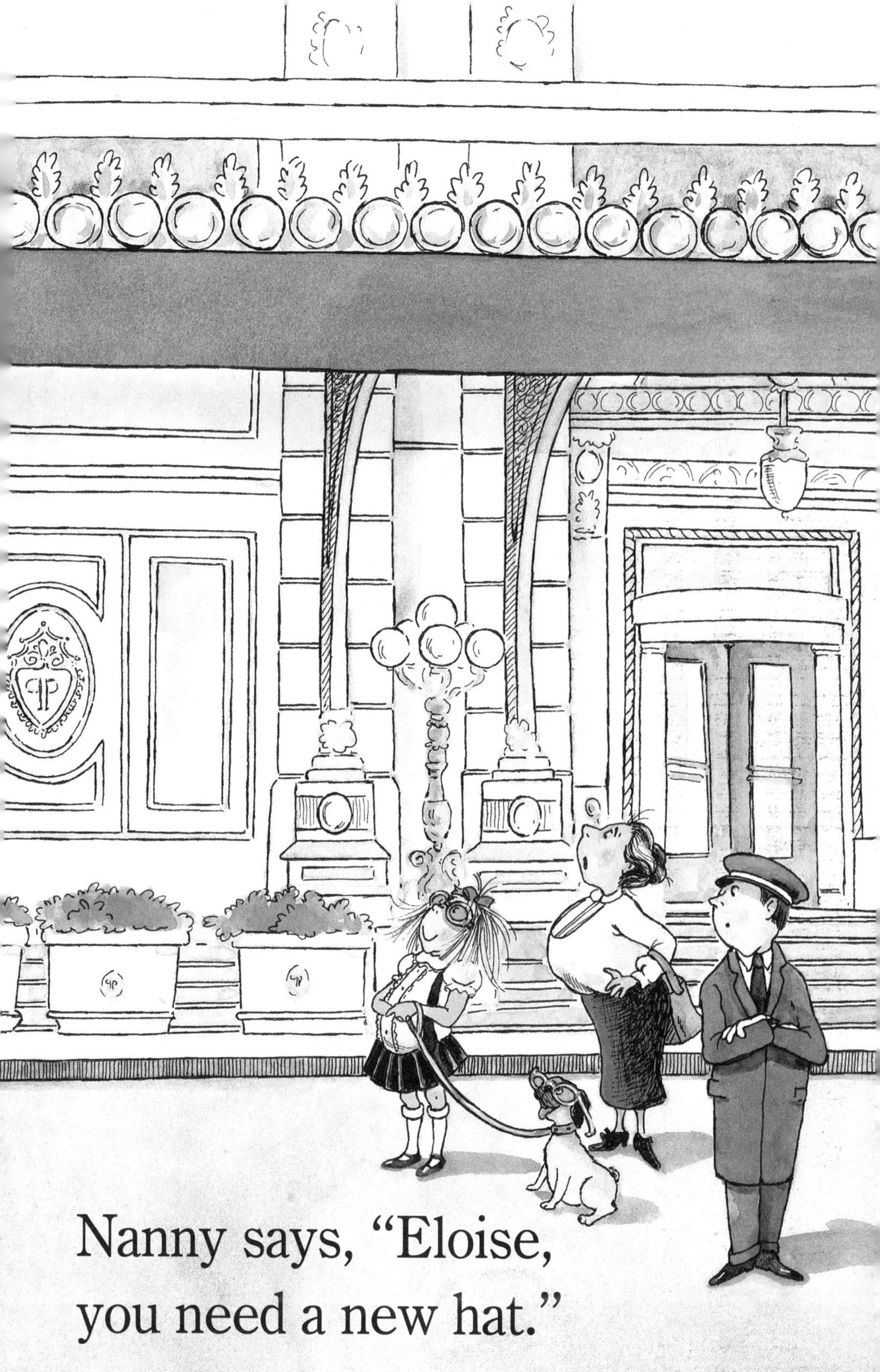

Nanny says, "Eloise,
you need a new hat."

Lampshades make
very good hats.

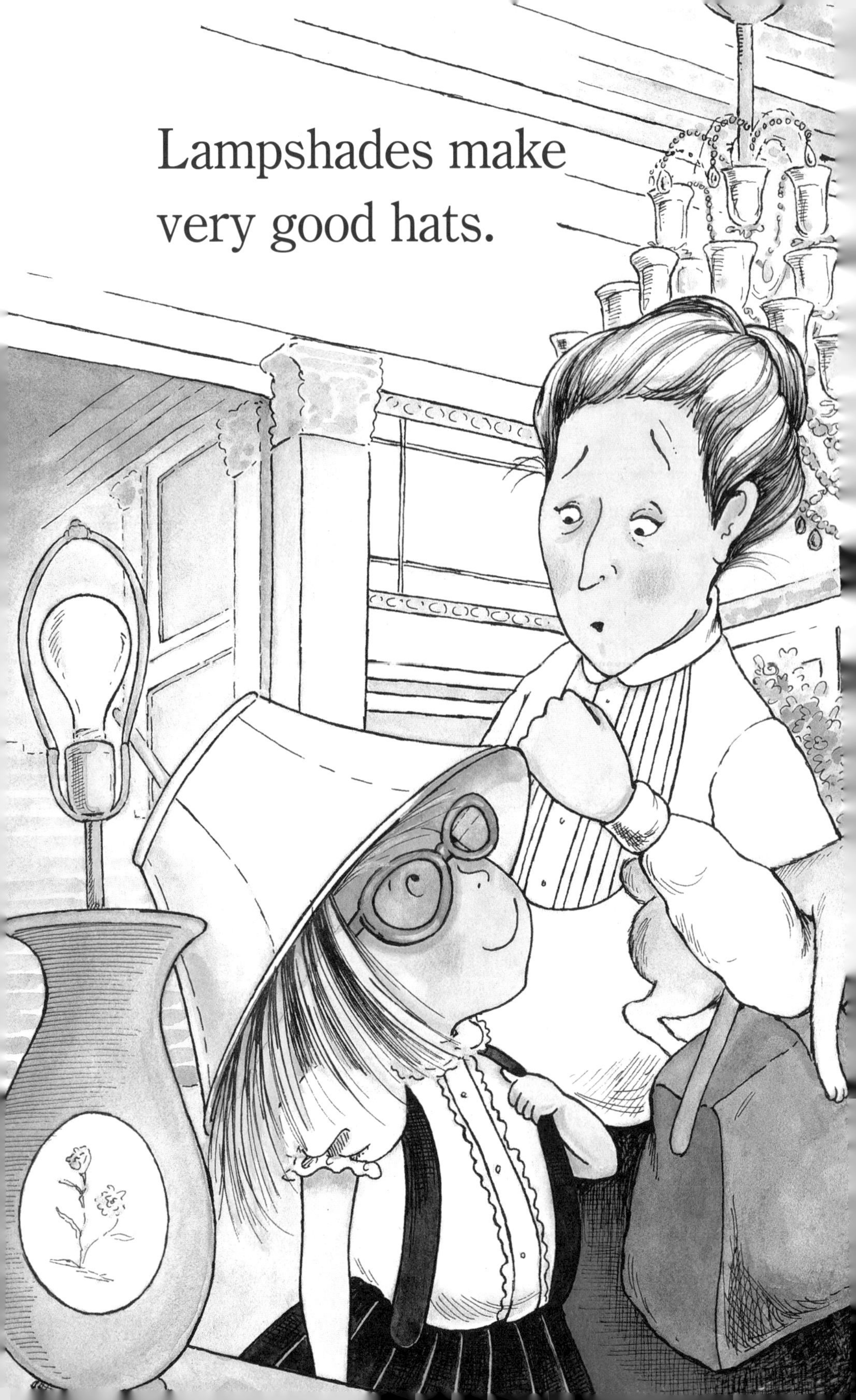

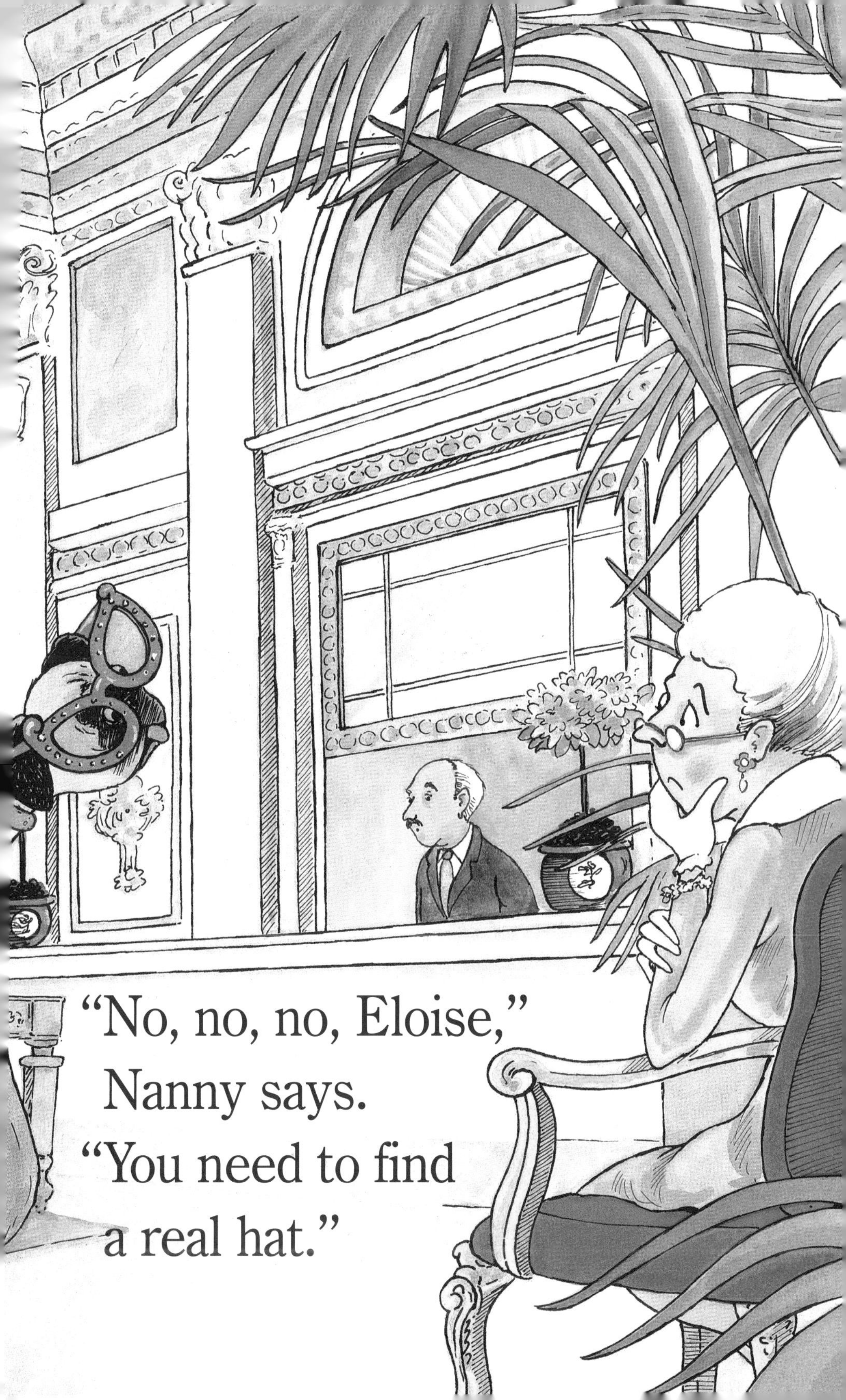

"No, no, no, Eloise,"
Nanny says.
"You need to find
a real hat."

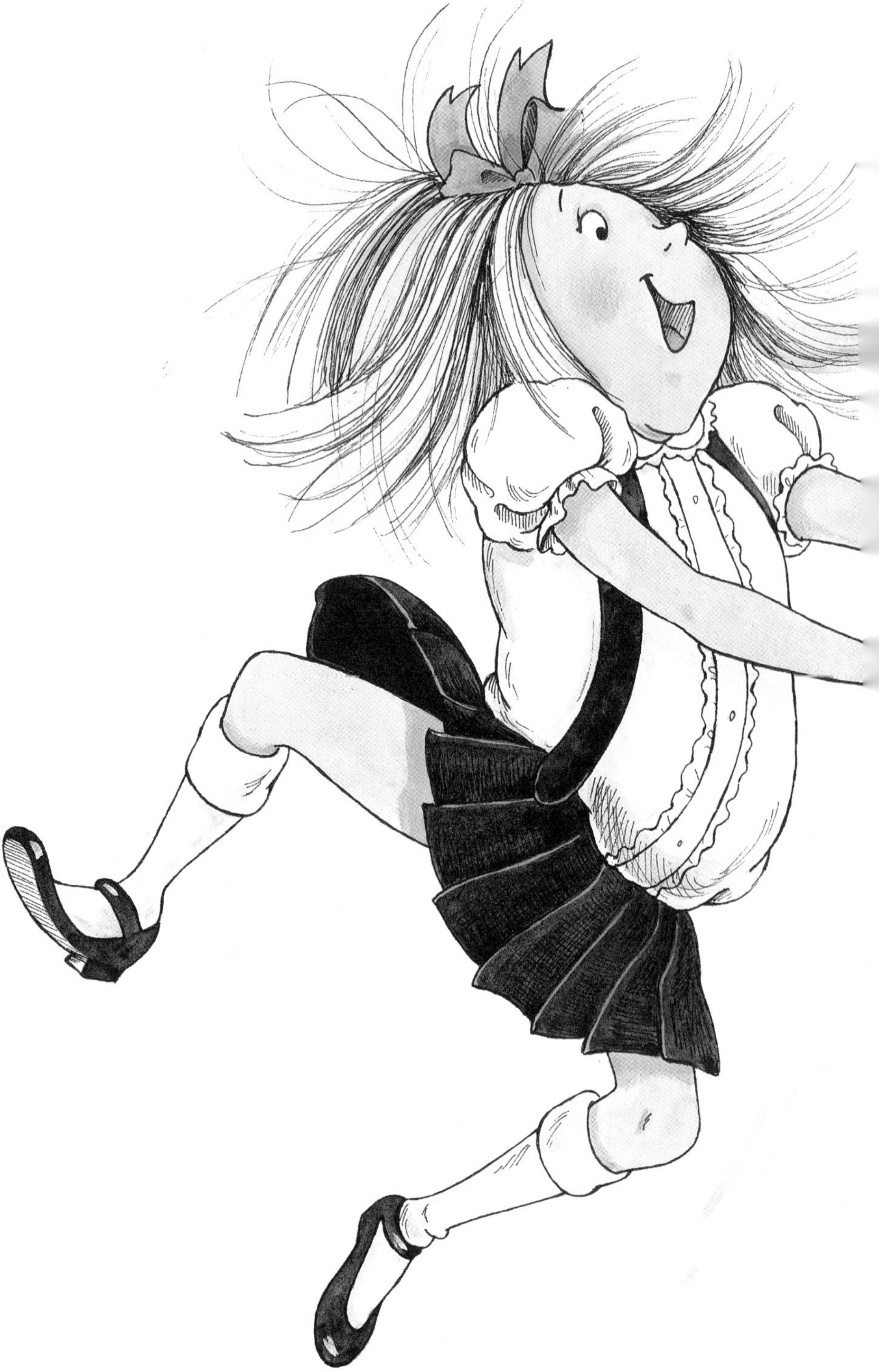

"I know where to find
a real hat," I say.
"I will visit the kitchen."

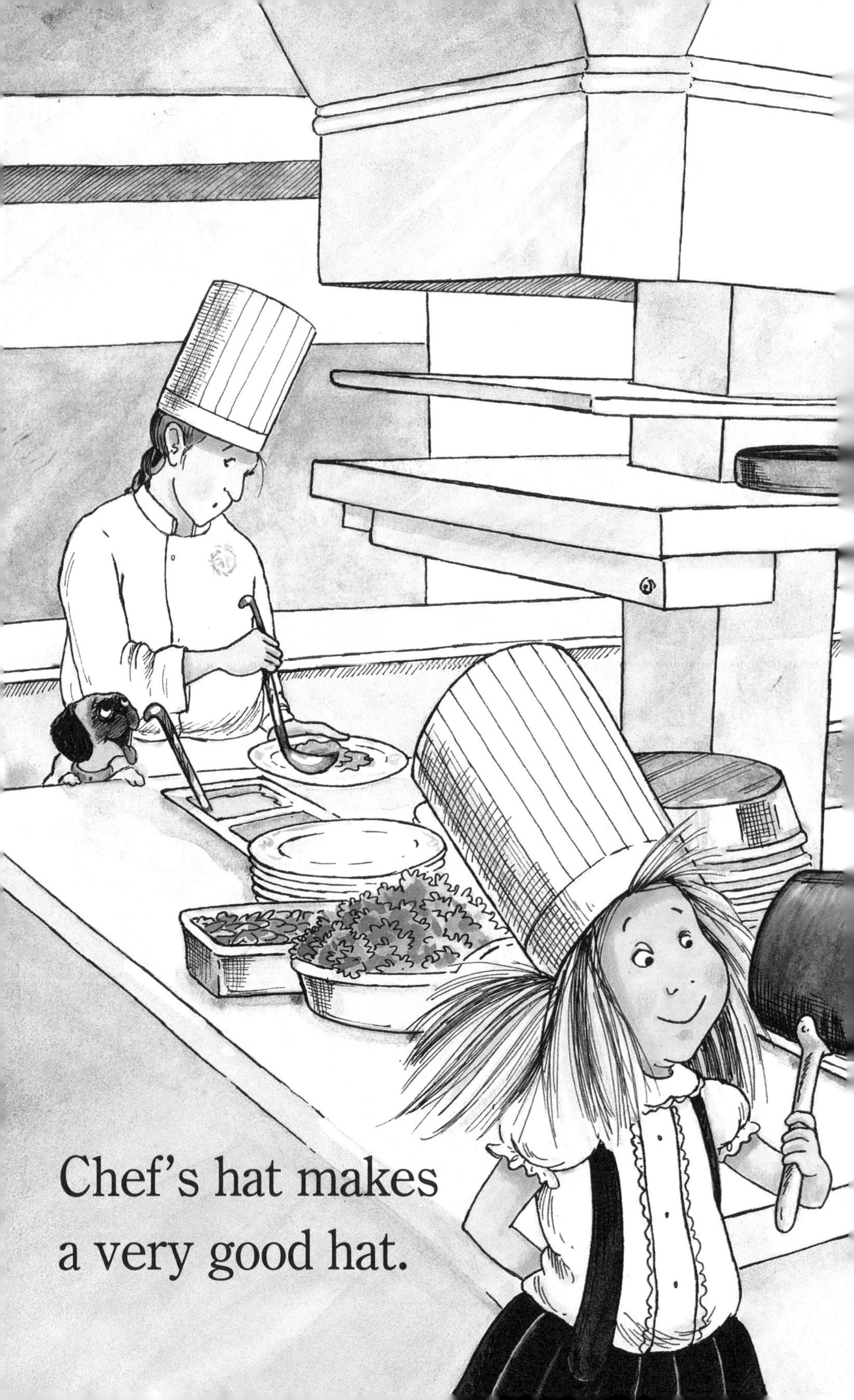

Chef's hat makes
a very good hat.

"No, no, no, Eloise,"
Nanny says.
"That hat is too tall."

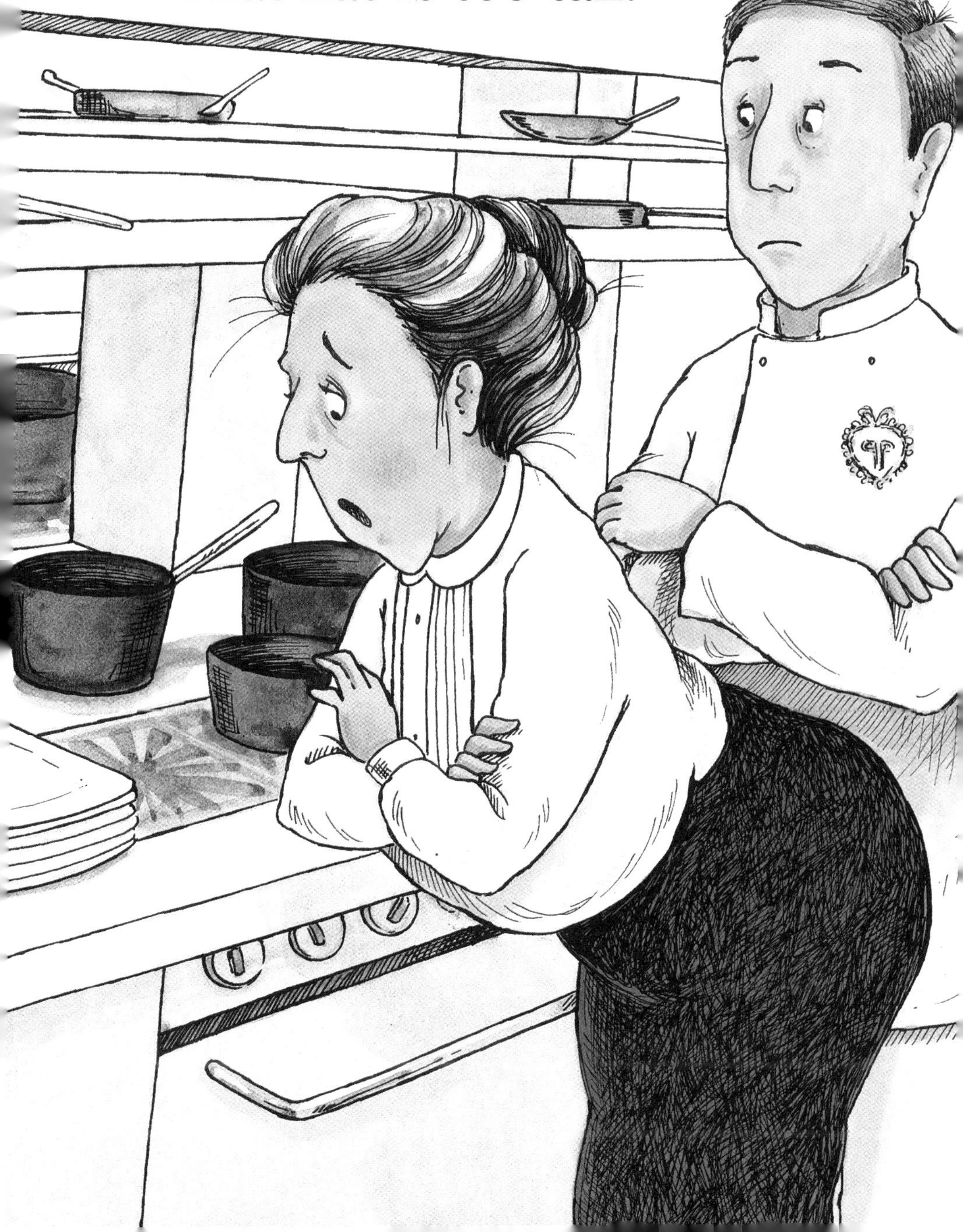

"I know," I say. "I will visit room service."

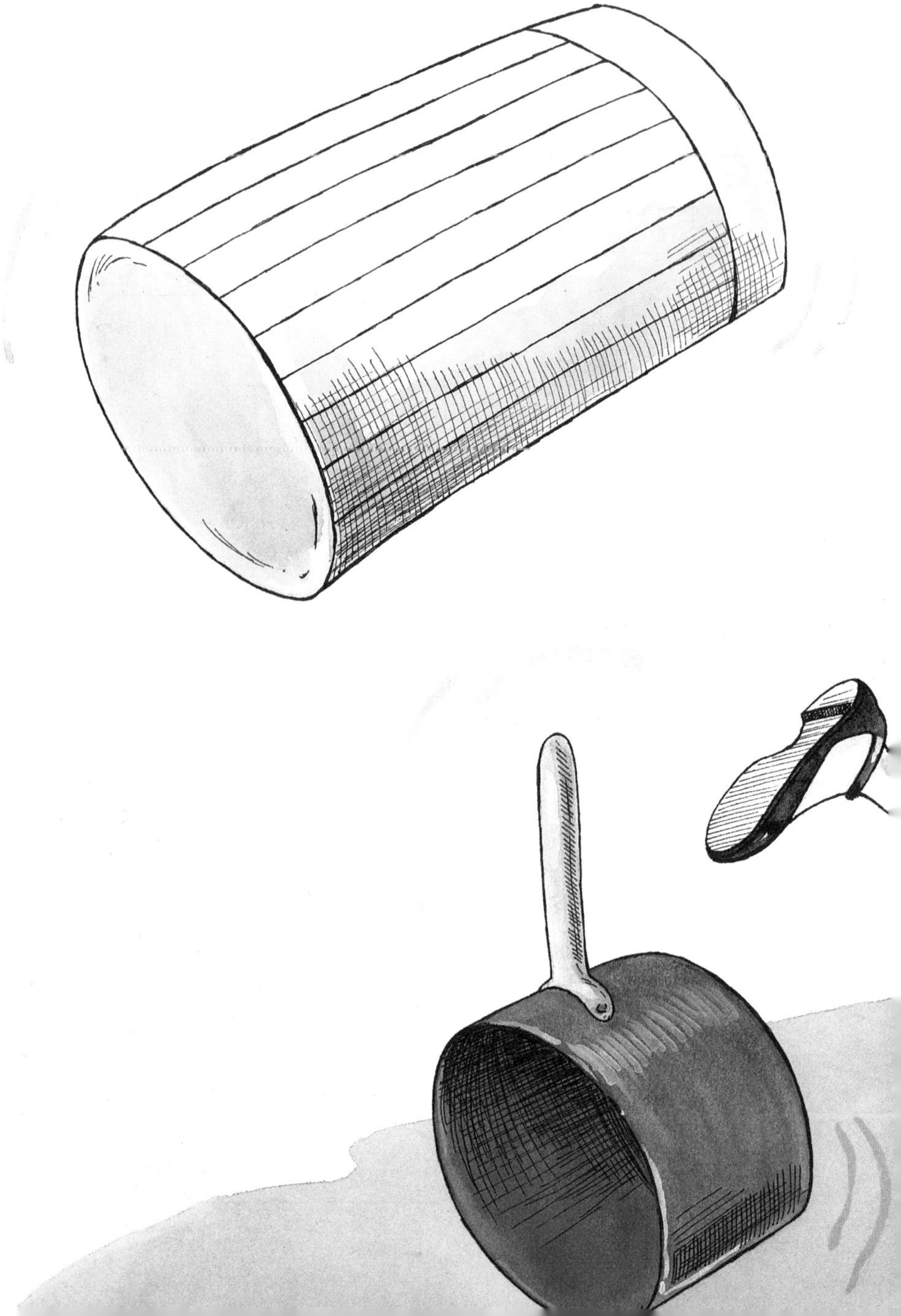

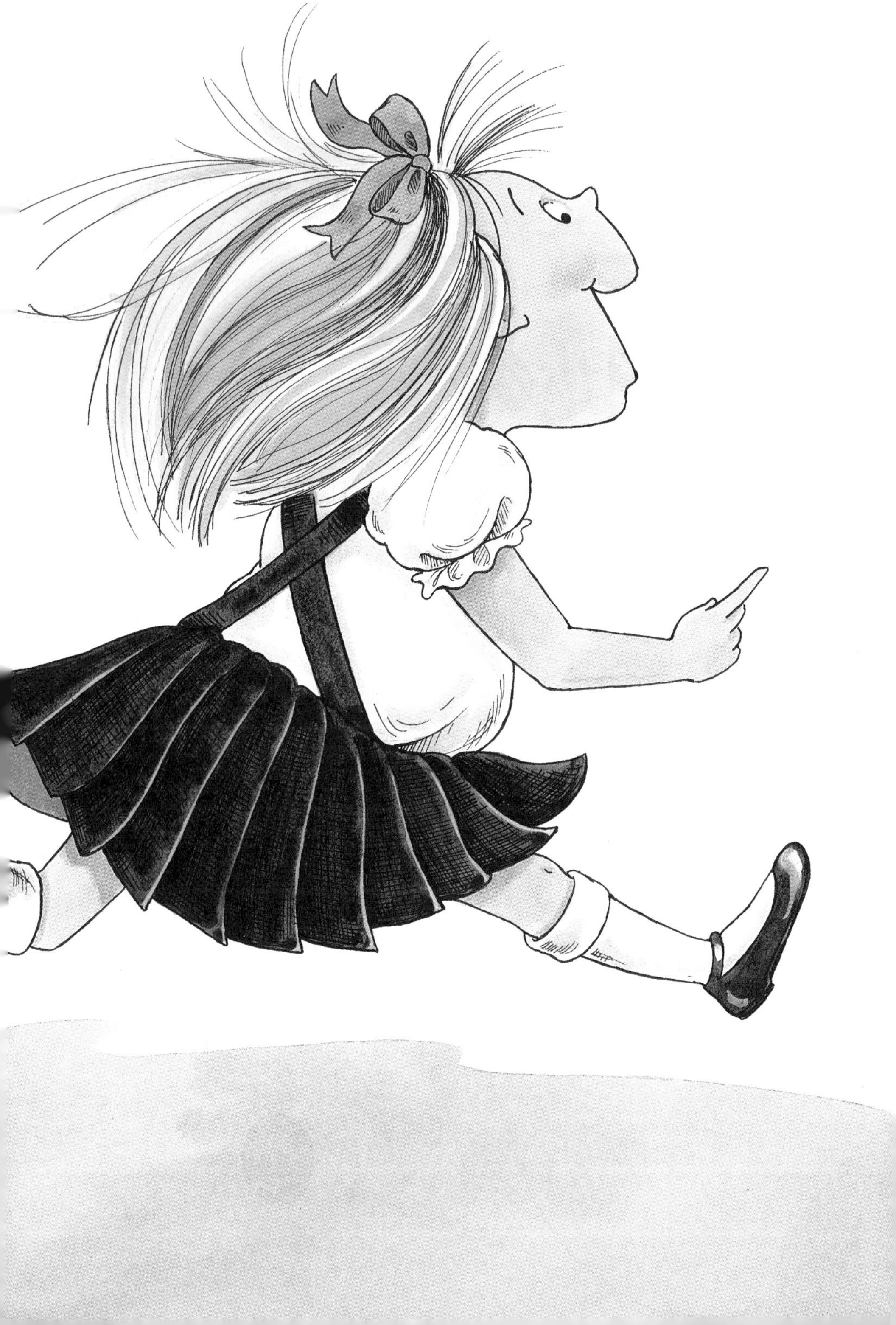

Room service hats
make very good hats.

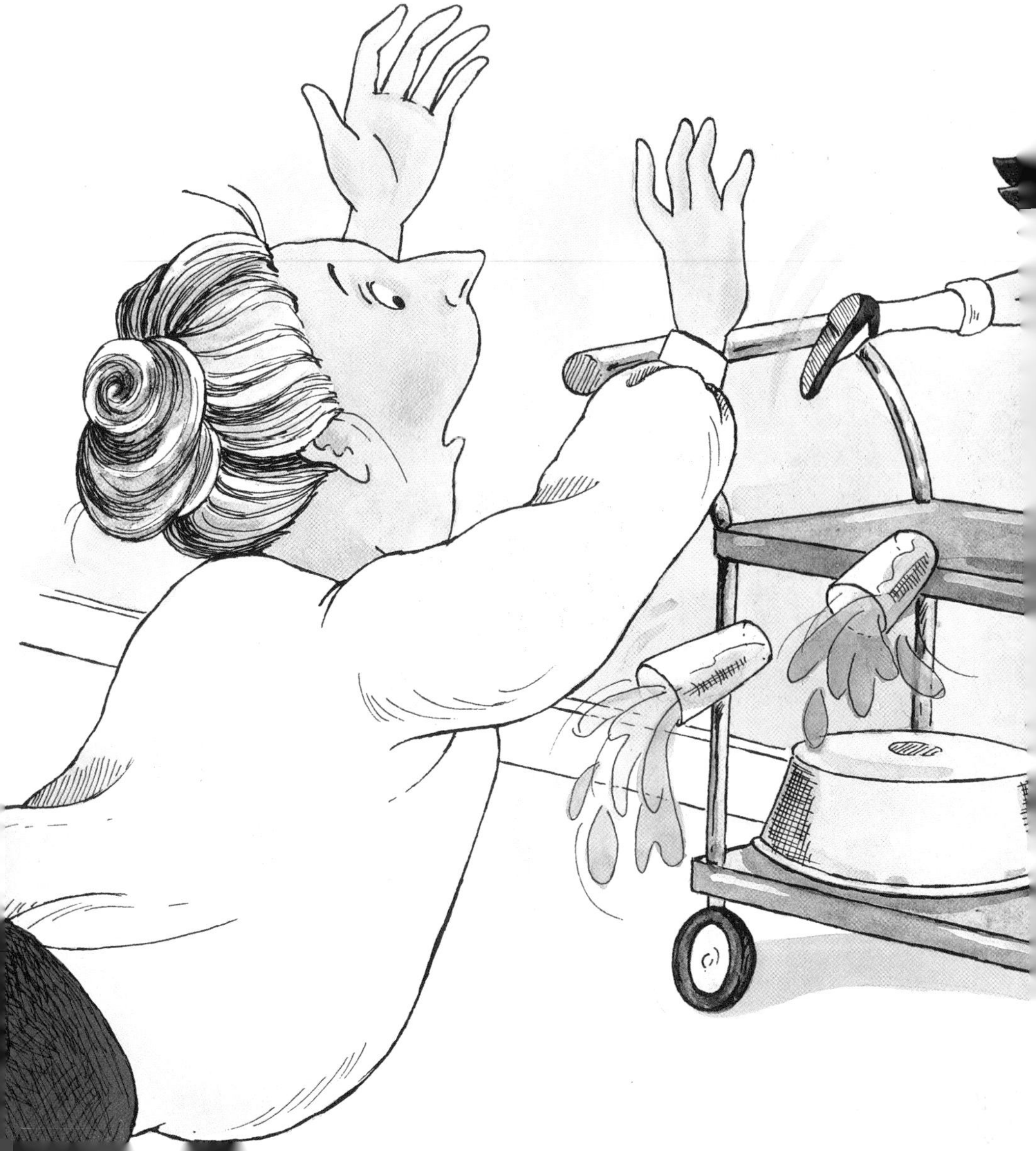

"No, no, no, Eloise,"
Nanny says.
"That hat has no brim."

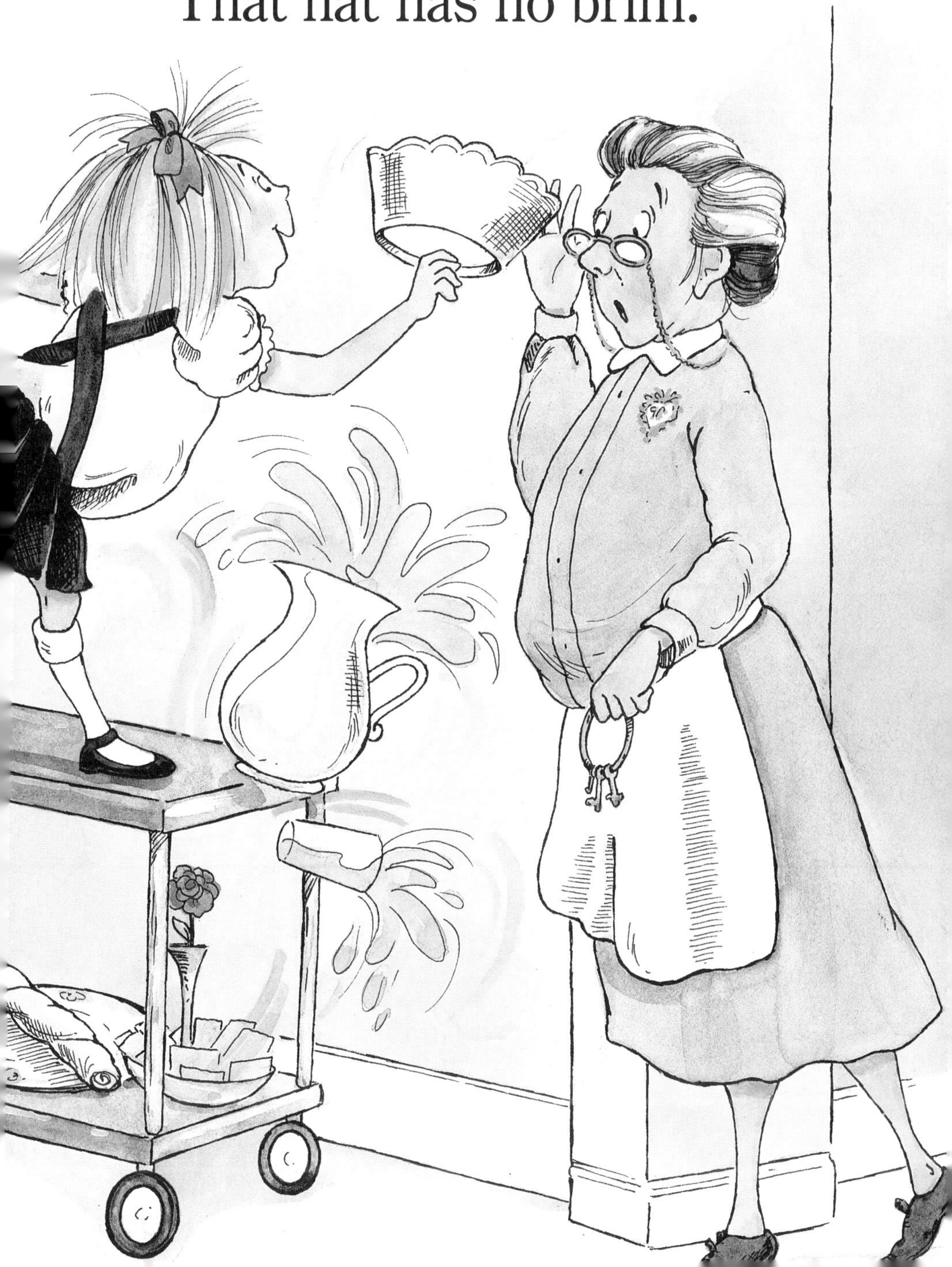

"Hmm," I say.
"I will visit
    the bell captain!"

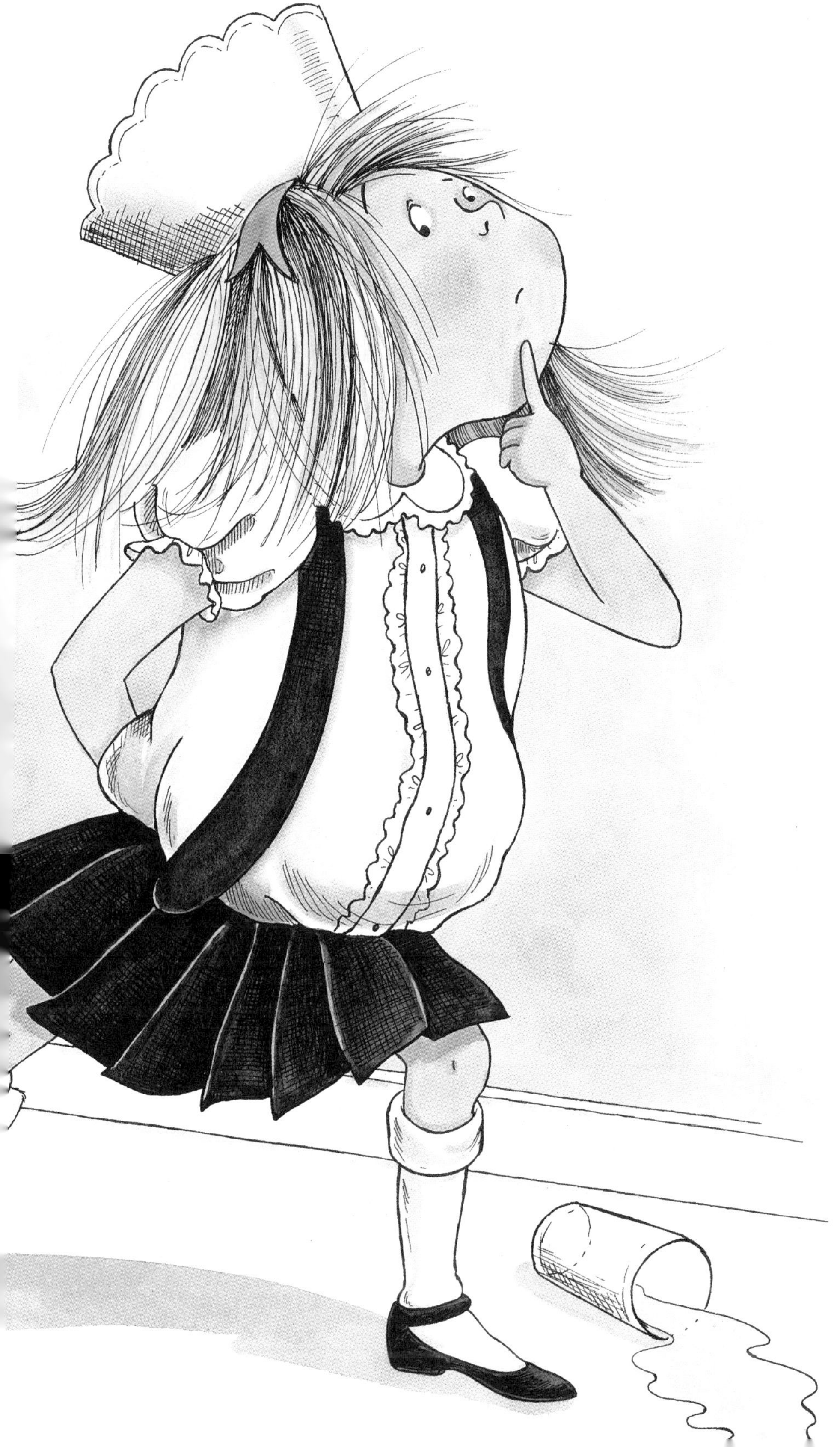

Bell captain hats
make very good hats.

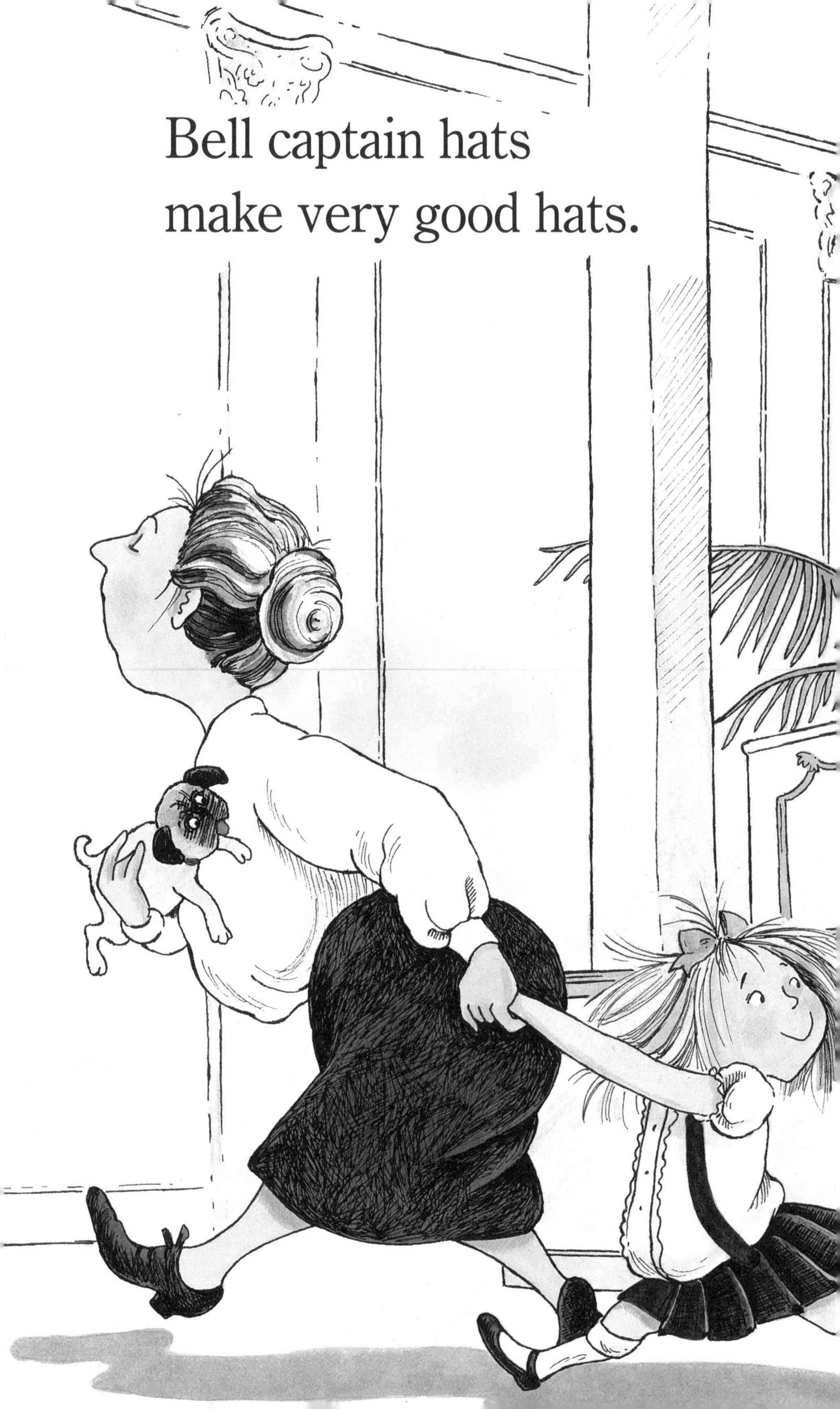

"No, no, no, Eloise,"
Nanny says.
"We need a hat
that is a pretty color."

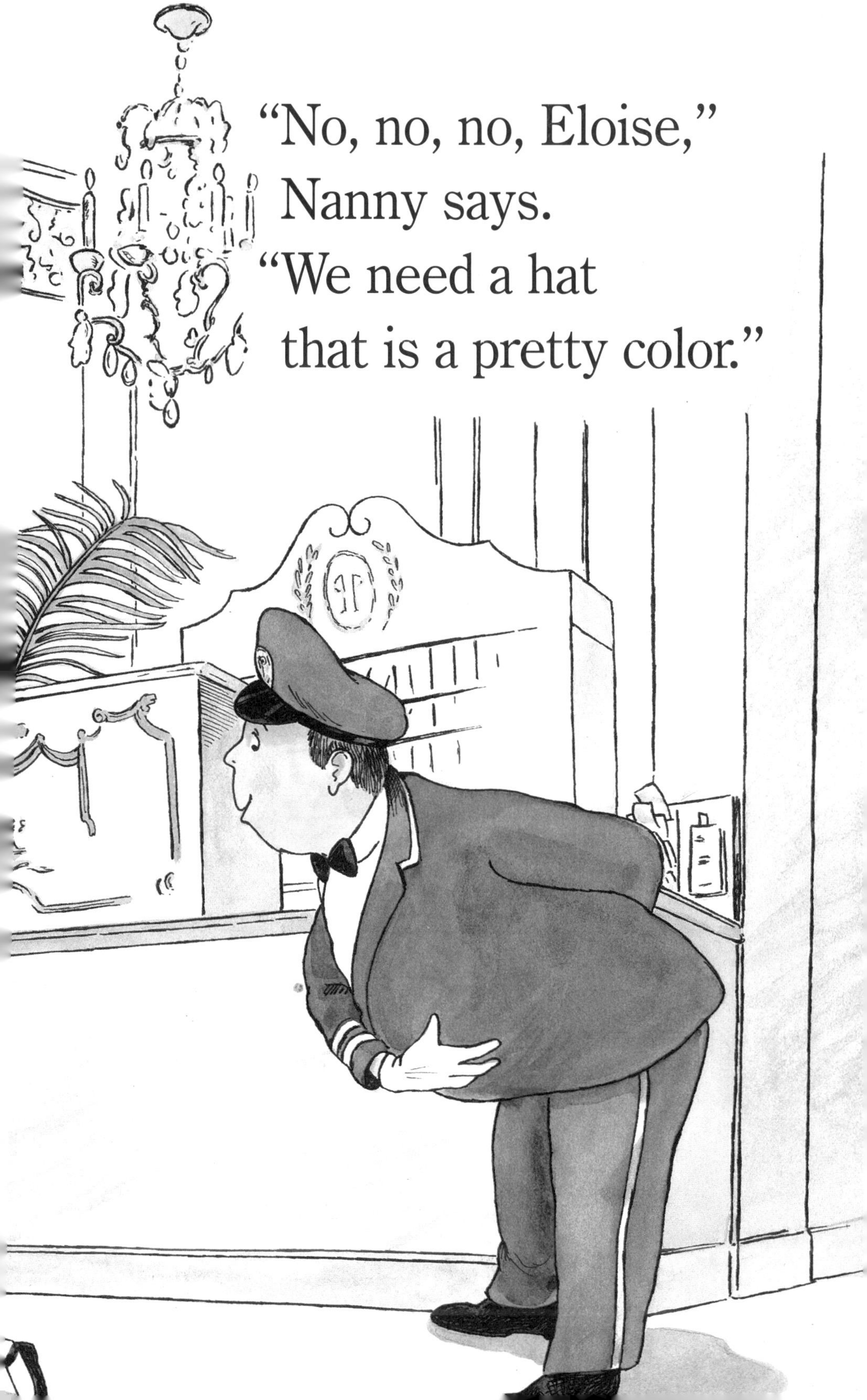

I visit the lobby.
There are hats everywhere!

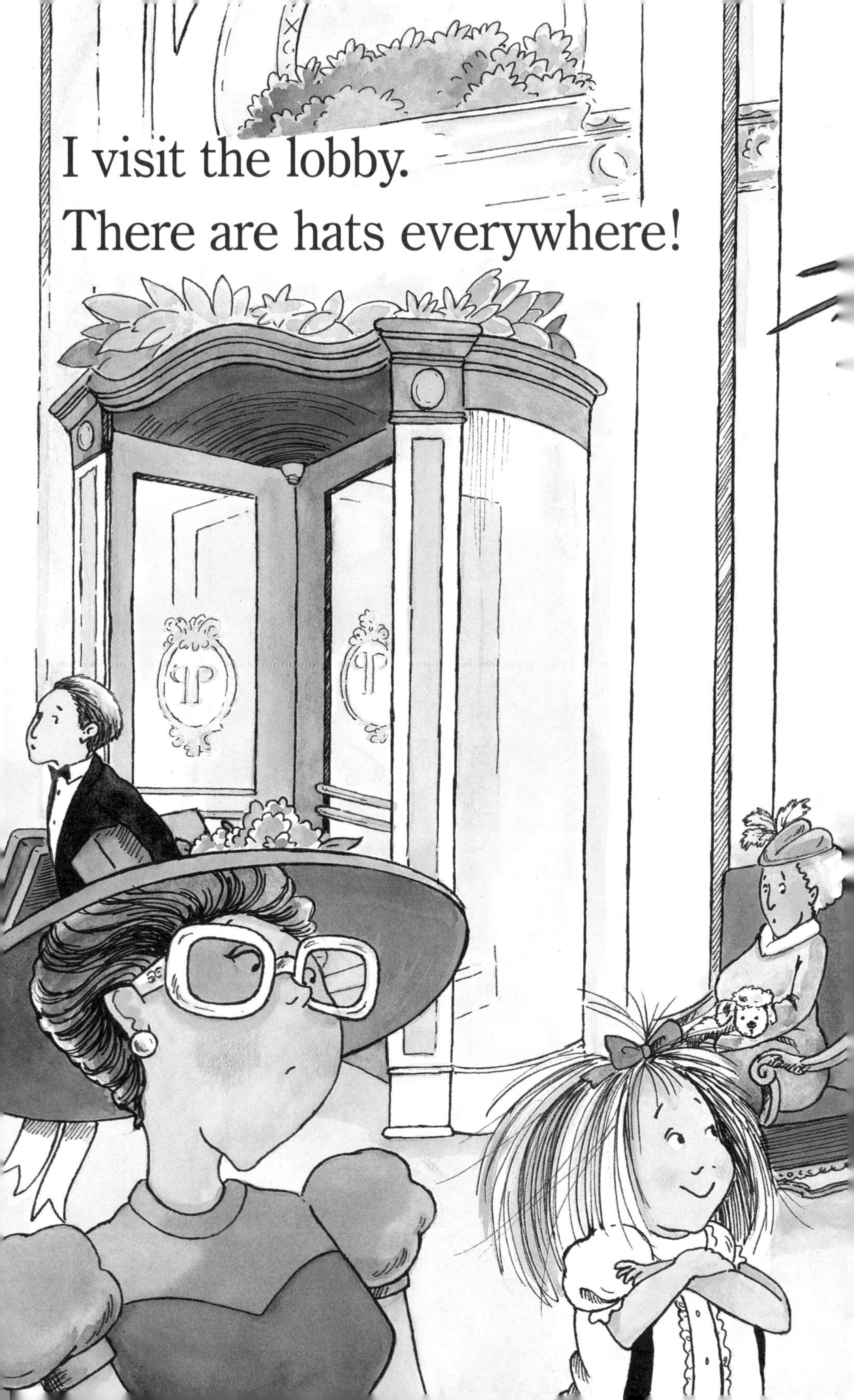

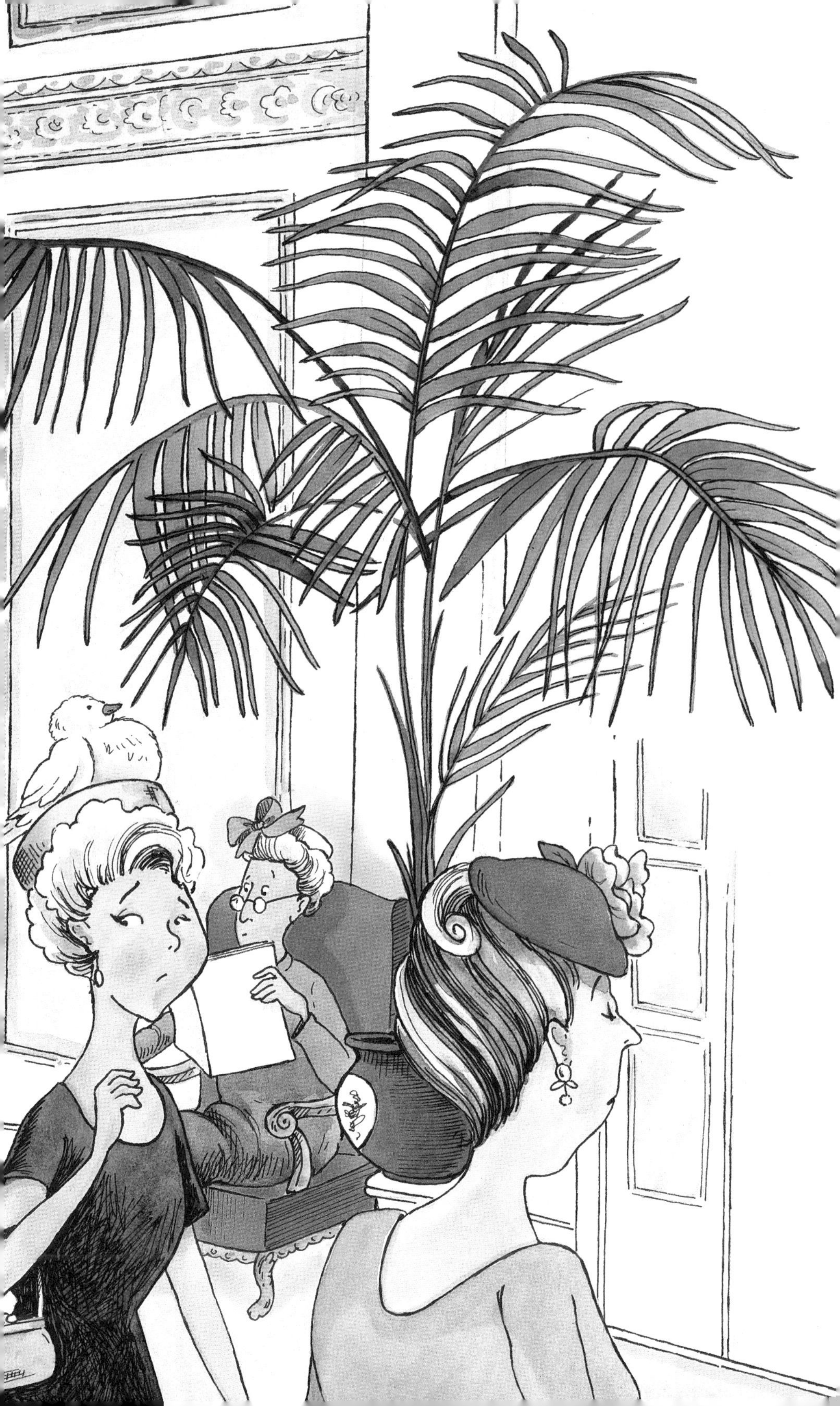

I try on a lady's hat.
It is a pretty color,
and it has a bird on top.
"Perfect," I say.

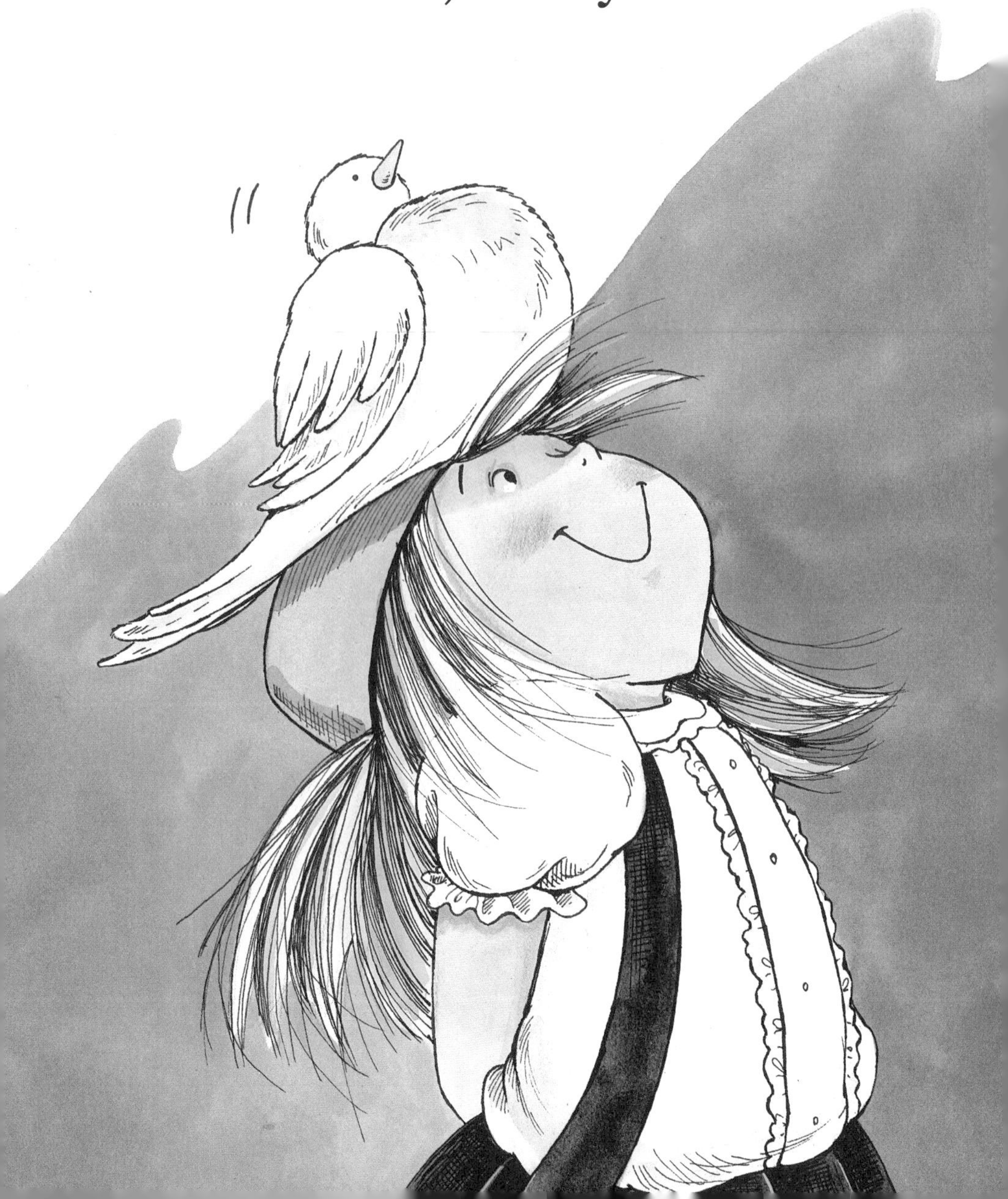

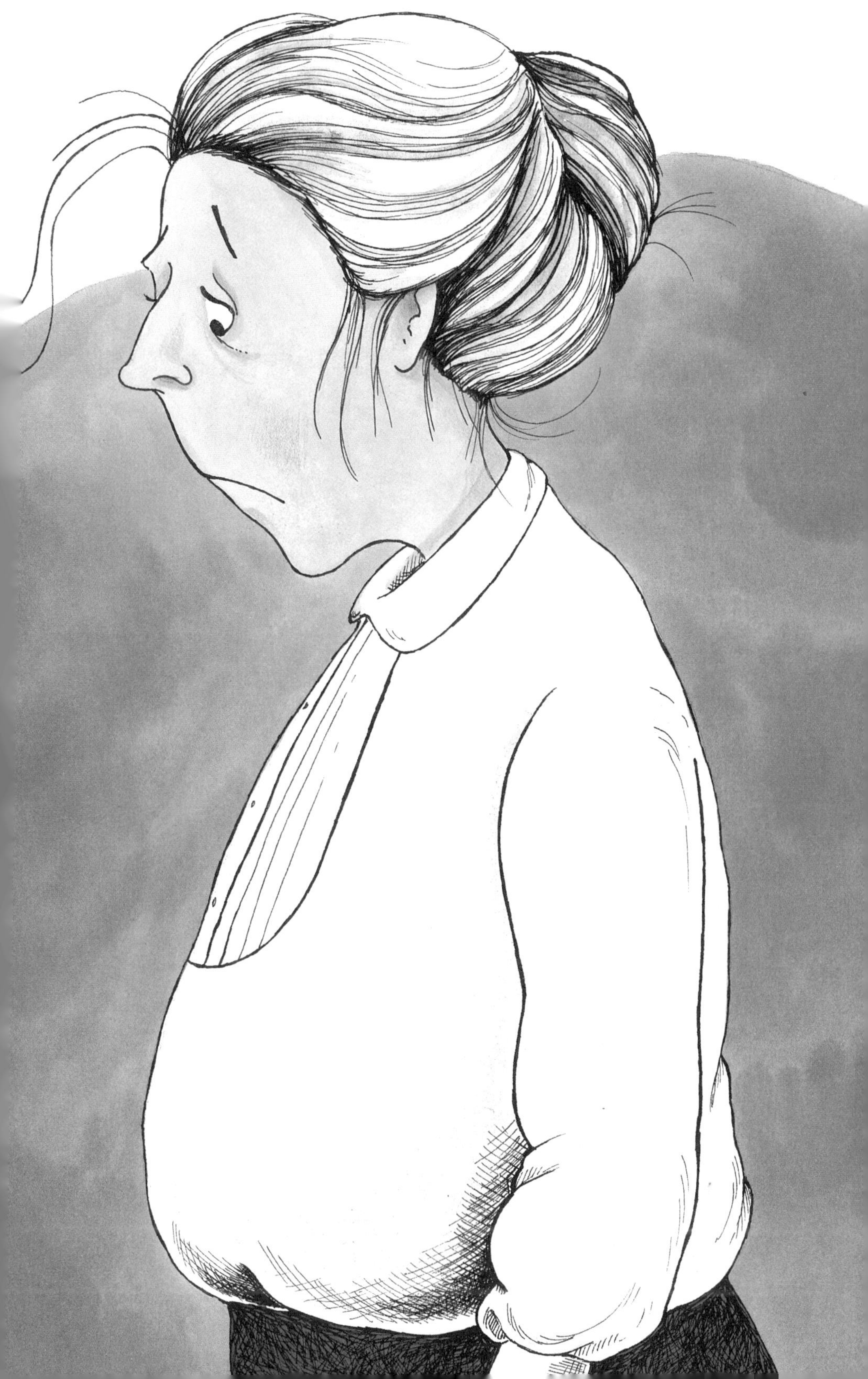

Nanny and the manager
do not agree.

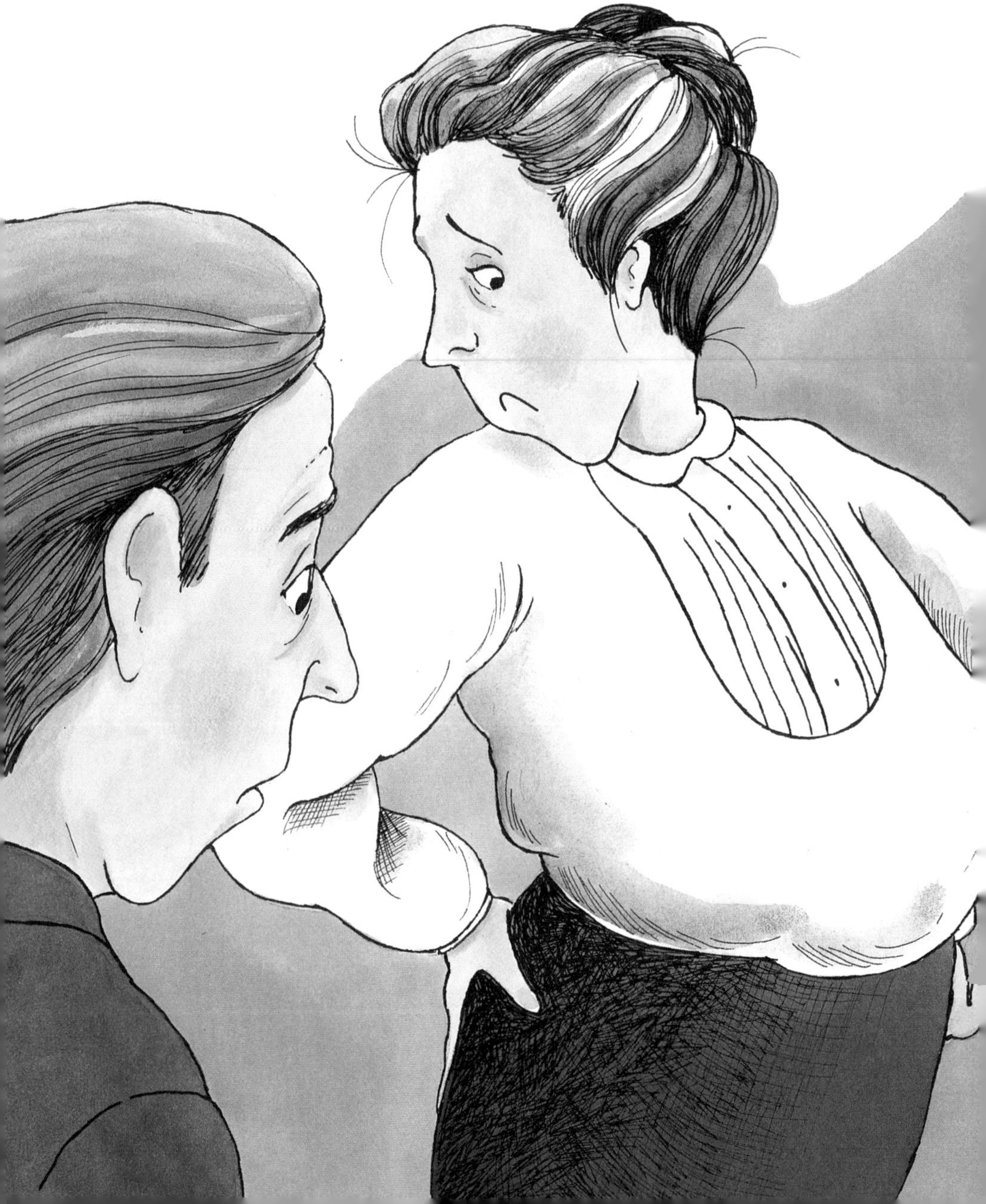

"Please give the lady
her hat back,"
Nanny says.

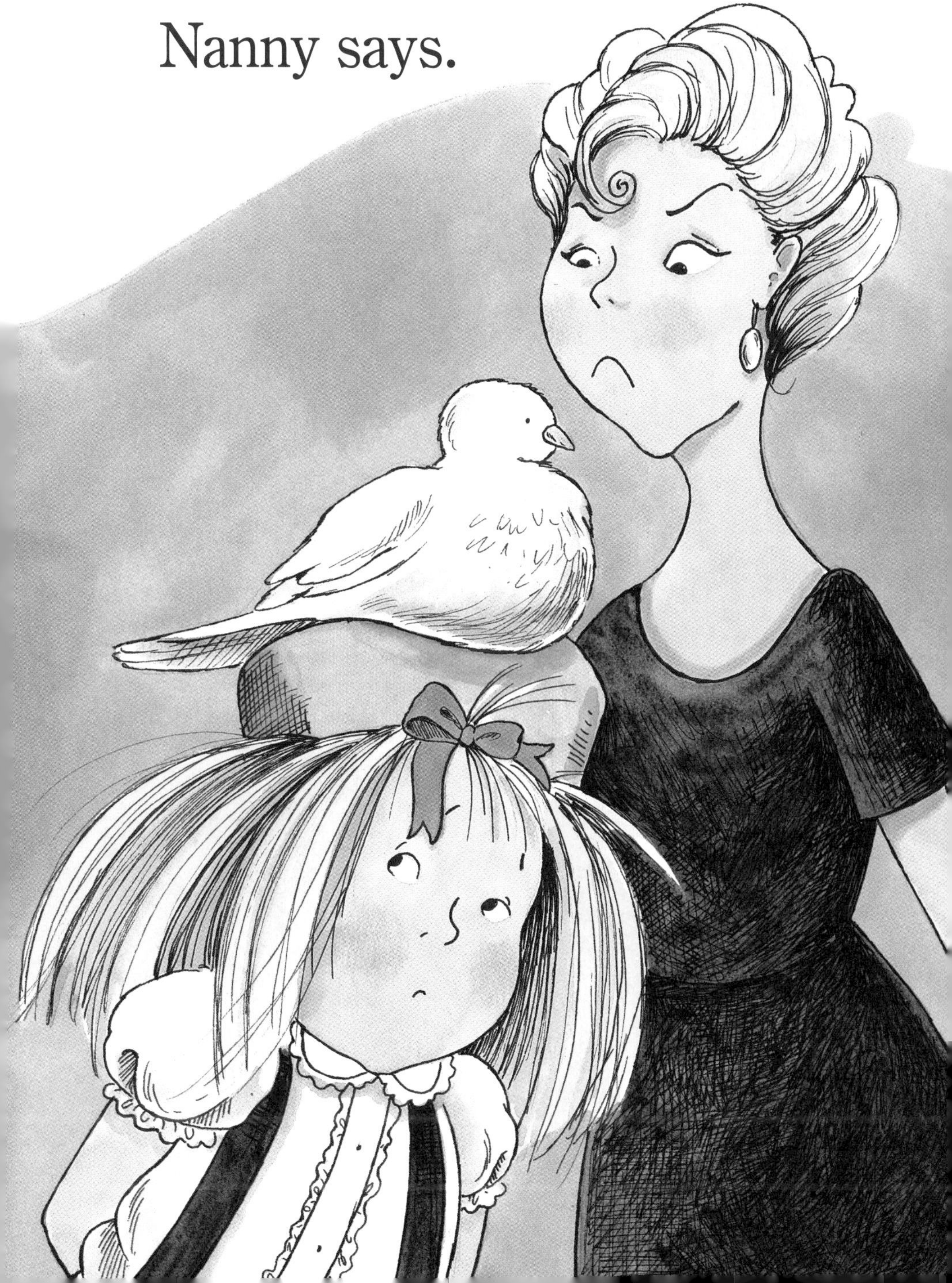

"Sorry."

"Eloise, I have a surprise,"
Nanny says.
She hands me a box.

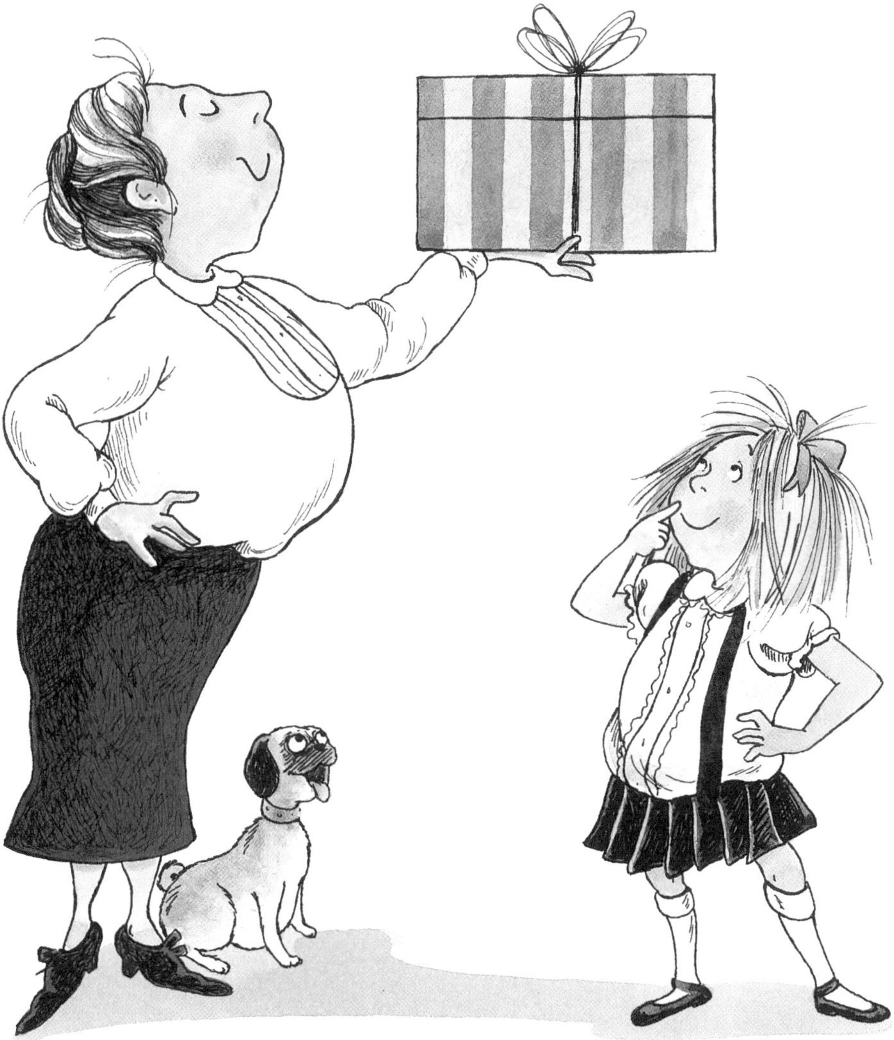

Inside is a new hat
just for me.

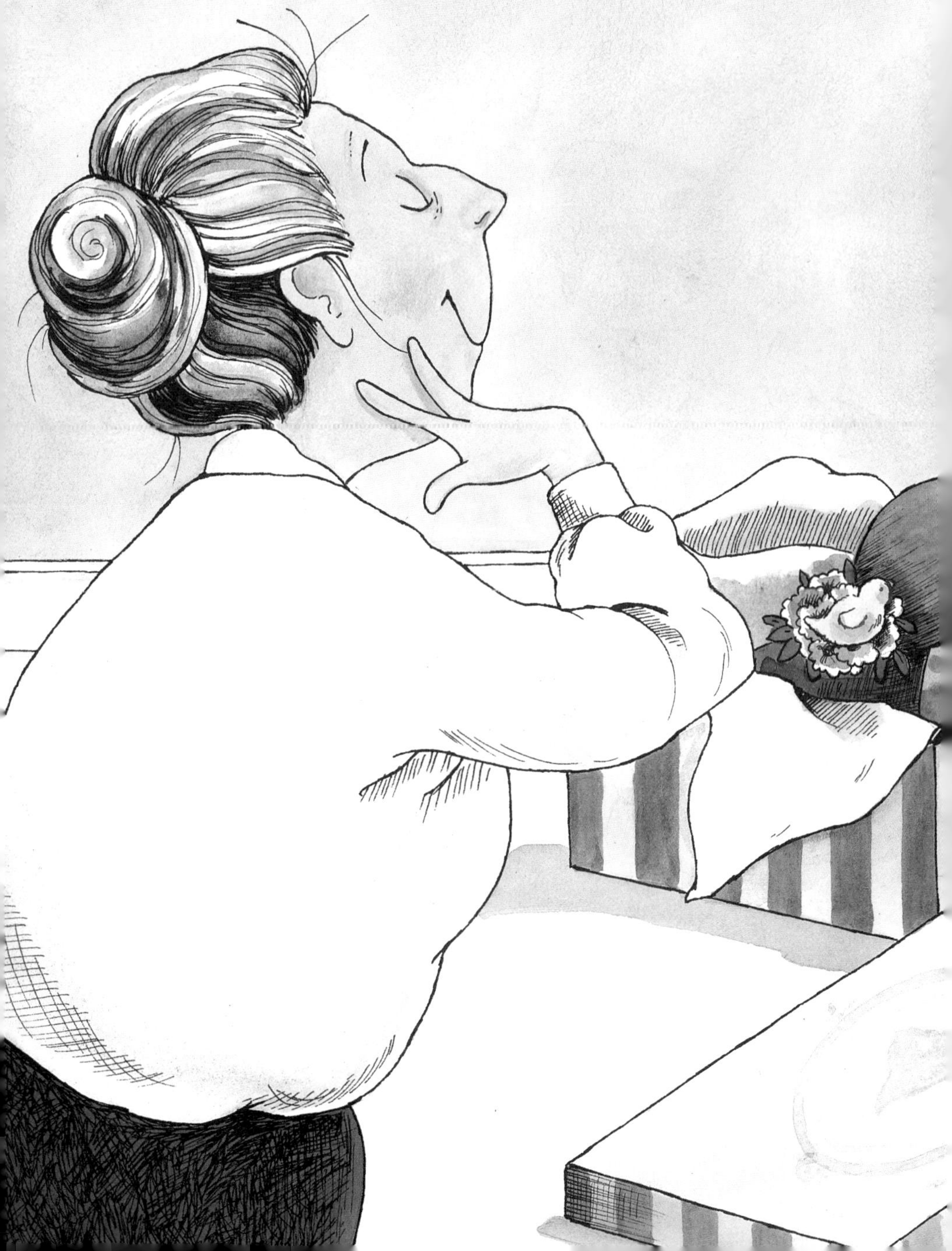

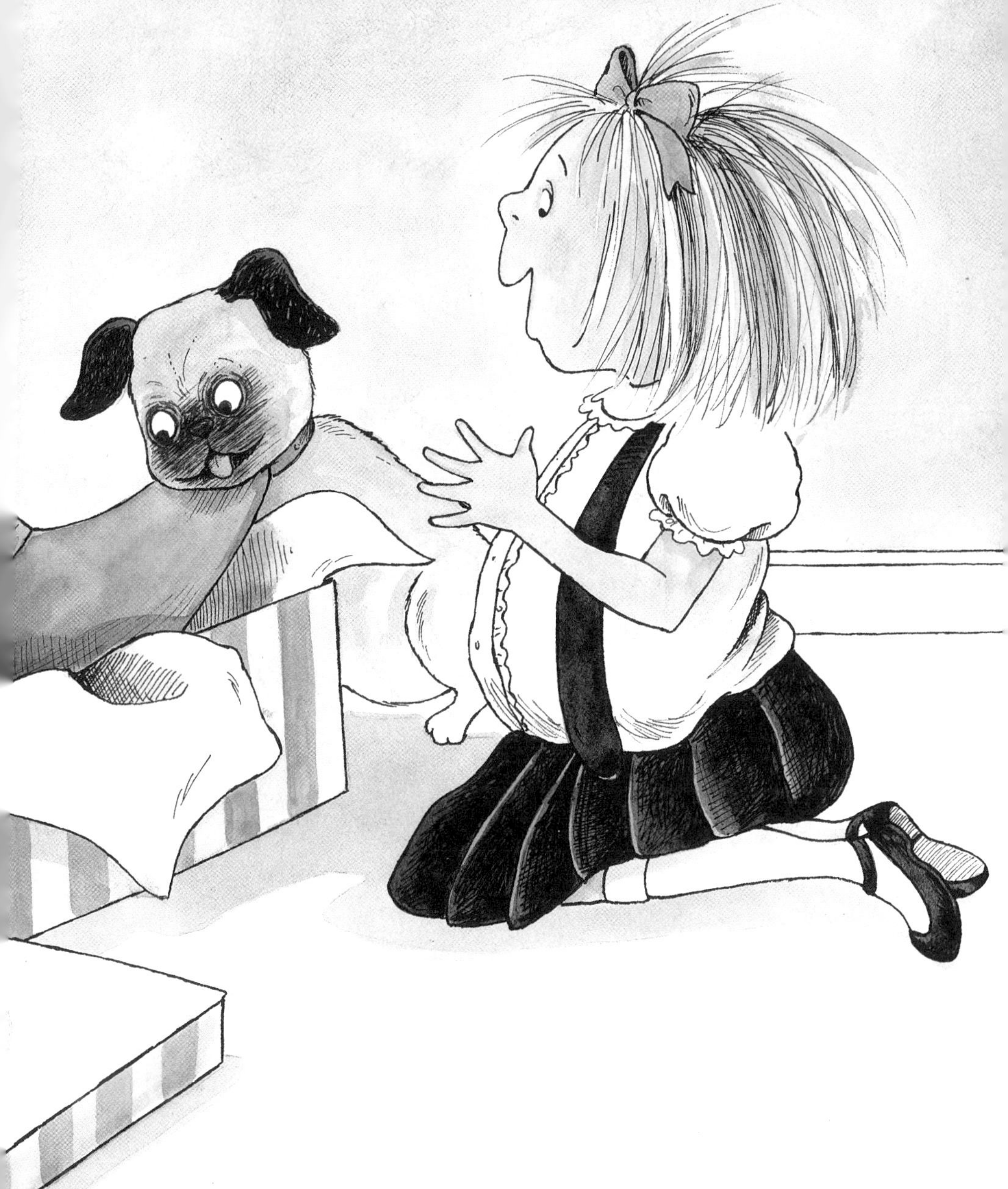

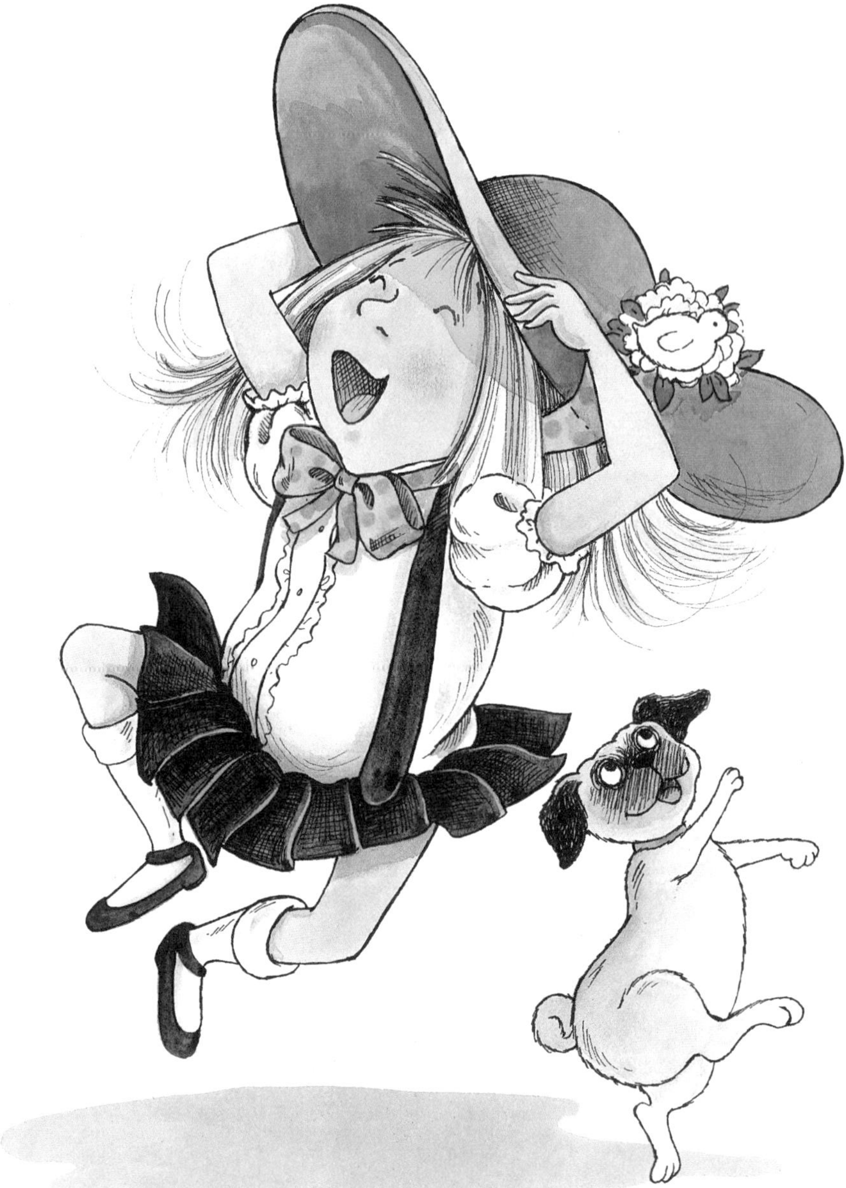

Oh, I love, love, love hats!